Deadbolts and Dinkles

by Kathy Kennedy Tapp
illustrated by Carol Newsom

This book is for Allie
— K.K.T.

To my husband Tom
who was willing to put on a pair of overalls
to help me with the book.
— C. N.

Text copyright © 2000 by Kathy Kennedy Tapp
Illustrations copyright © 2000 by Carol Newsom

For information contact:

MONDO Publishing
990 Avenue of the Americas
New York, NY 10019

Visit our web site at http://www.mondopub.com

Printed in the United States of America

00 01 02 03 04   9 8 7 6 5 4 3 2 1

Design by Eliza Green
Production by The Kids at Our House

Library of Congress Cataloging-in-Publication Data
Tapp. Kathy Kennedy
  Deadbolts and dinkles / by Kathy Kennedy Tapp ; illustrated by
Carol Newsom.
     p.   cm.
  Summary: When his mother has car trouble, Zach is afraid that he will be
stranded at his grandfather's new apartment with his younger brother, instead of
going to his friend's sleepover birthday party.
     ISBN 1-57255-774-5
     [1. Grandfathers–Fiction. 2. Brothers–Fiction. 3. Moving, Household–Fiction.]
I. Newsom, Carol, ill. II. Title.
PZ7. T1646 Dd 2000
[Fic]–dc21   99 - 049401
                                                                    CIP
                                                                    AC

Contents

The Deadbolt Party

"Zach, we're going to start the party! Where are you?" Tyler's voice yelled into the phone.

"I'm right here, like I told you," I yelled back. "In my grandpa's new apartment."

I looked around the bare room. No rugs, no furniture, just some boxes, and my little brother BJ sliding around the bare floor on a pillow. Mom left an hour ago to get one more load of Grandpa's stuff. She was SUPPOSED to be back by now, to drive me to the party.

"Trevor's here and we want to cut the cake–"

"DON'T CUT IT YET! I'll BE there. My mom will be

back any minute!" I talked fast and loud, trying to convince him.

They couldn't start the sleepover without me! We'd been planning it for weeks. It was Tyler's birthday, but I came up with most of the ideas—like having a cake decorated with a lock and key and handcuffs, and the three of us sleeping outside in the tent with our flashlights and antiburglar supplies.

"Well, HURRY," Tyler muttered. "We can't just hang around forever, you know."

"Yeah. She'll be here. Any second."

"Deadbolts. Over and out," Tyler whispered.

"Signing off. Deadbolts," I whispered back. It was our secret password. And our club name. Deadbolts.

"I want to go home." BJ was whining again. "There's nothing to do."

I put the phone back on the hook and ran into the living room.

"Mom will be back pretty soon."

"Where's Mommy?" BJ put his thumb in his mouth.

I sighed. "She went to get more of Grandpa's stuff. It's all in Aunt Margaret's garage, remember?"

"I want to go home." BJ's lip started quivering and his face scrunched up. "I want to watch my TV show. It wasn't over." He gave up on me and ran to the other side of the room, where Grandpa was unpacking some pans. "I want to watch the unicorns!"

"The TV isn't here yet," Grandpa said, giving BJ a little pat on the head. But his voice was sort of growling, and his eyebrows seemed like one bristly white line over his eyes, he was frowning so hard.

Back in Michigan he would have said something like, "Oh, come on now, BJ! We can think of something else fun to do!" And he would have, too. He used to let me take pictures with his camera, and he made fun toys for BJ, and we camped out sometimes, in his old army tent.

But not now. He was walking into the kitchen. Stomping is more like it. "Who needs so many cupboards? Must be fifteen if there's one. And this place has so many shiny counters, it looks like a hospital."

I don't think Grandpa wants to be in this new apartment anymore than me or BJ. But since he fell and hurt his hip last spring, he can't take care of his farm in Michigan anymore. So he moved to California, to live closer to us.

"I want to go home." BJ tugged at my shirt. "I want my toys."

Three-year-olds are a PAIN. Especially when they don't have their naps. Then they're really cranky. I looked around. Maybe there was something he could play with in one of the boxes. I checked the label on the one closest to me, "Christmas decorations."

Great. Just what we needed in July. I checked the next box, "Kitchen." In my mind I saw a picture of Grandpa's red and white farmhouse kitchen squeezed up like an accordion inside the box.

The next box was labeled, "Shop."

"Grandpa, can I look inside this box?" Grandpa had neat stuff in his craft shop. I started pulling out the tucked-in flaps. "I'll be careful." I could already see pieces of wood and Grandpa's glue gun and other tools.

"I want to do it, too!" BJ started yanking at the box of ornaments.

The phone rang.

"I'll get it!" I ran into the hall.

It was Mom.

"Zach, there's something wrong with the car. I'm at a garage right now . . ."

"Mom! I've got to get to Tyler's party! They're waiting for me! I'm already late."

"I'm really sorry, Zach, but it looks like you'll have to miss Tyler's party."

Stranded at Grandpa's

"MOM!"

"Please don't yell in my ear, Zach." Mom really sounded tired and uptight. "This will take awhile. I'm lucky this garage gives emergency service. But you'll all need to eat something. Isn't there a Mini-mart down the block from the apartment?" Mom's voice went on and on, worrying. I hardly listened. Of course I was hungry. I was supposed to have pizza pretty soon. And ice cream. And cake.

"Zach! Are you listening?"

"Mom–Tyler's party. I've got to go!"

"Believe me, Zach, I don't like this anymore than you do. Put Grandpa on." Mom was using her don't-argue-

with-me voice.

Life was not fair.

Well, I wasn't giving up. No way. Maybe I'd get to the party late, but I'd get there.

"Now just quit your worrying, Jenny, and take care of that car." Grandpa sounded gruff and stiff, talking to Mom on the phone. "The boys and I can manage just fine."

No we couldn't. We didn't WANT to.

"A taxi!" Grandpa just about snorted the word. "You will not call a taxi. Don't call anyone. We are FINE. Do you think I'm helpless?"

BJ ran over to me. He was holding a plastic reindeer. A string of Christmas tree lights trailed behind him, caught in the laces of his sneaker.

"Put Grandpa's ornaments back," I yelled. "Leave those decorations alone!"

BJ started crying loudly.

"What?" Grandpa hollered into the phone. "What did you say, Jenny? Some place to eat? Now listen here, these hips are perfectly capable of walking two blocks."

Grandpa put the phone down and started toward the door. "Now," he said, picking up BJ. His voice was really a growl. I NEVER heard Grandpa sound so grouchy. "Sandwiches and milk," he barked. "OUT."

No Pizza, No Cake

The Mini-mart was two blocks away.

We bought cheese sandwiches and ham sandwiches wrapped in plastic and a quart of milk from the refrigerator section. Grandpa set BJ down on the checkout counter with the milk and sandwiches.

"I want candy!" BJ cried, waving a bag of gumdrops in the air. He gave a big yank on the paper and gumdrops shot all over the counter. A red one hit the clerk.

"Hold onto him while I pay, Zach," Grandpa ordered. As I grabbed BJ, I read the sign over the cash register: "For security reasons, we don't give change for bills over $20."

I looked at the clerk. He was a teenager. Was he afraid of being robbed? Was he afraid someone would come in here and take all the money from his cash register?

I know about stuff like this. Tyler and Trevor do, too. That's why we call ourselves the Deadbolts. Whenever I go into new places, I always check them out. Some places are safer than others. Some have good locks. Once our class went on a field trip to the art museum. Everyone else asked questions about the pictures and statues. But I spent all my time talking to the security guards, asking them about their burglar alarms.

I looked around the Mini-mart. No guards in grocery stores. Not very safe at all.

"What would you do if someone came in and wanted to rob you?" I asked the clerk. He stopped ringing up the sandwiches.

"What?"

"What would you do if someone wanted to rob you? Would you call the police? Do you have a burglar alarm?" I asked.

"So are you thinking of robbing the store?" he said in a not very friendly voice.

"No, but I'm interested in this sort of stuff. What

14

would you do?" I said again, bouncing up and down a little. It's really exciting, thinking about it all.

He put everything we bought in a bag. "Yeah, I'd call the police," he said in a real low, mysterious voice. "And they'd come and grab the guy. . ."

"But if you didn't get a chance to call. . ."

"Then I'd get your little brother to throw gumdrops at him."

"I'm *serious*!"

"You know what? You better not ask all these kinds of questions if you're ever in an airport. They'll arrest you."

"My grandson has quite an imagination," Grandpa said. He handed the bag to me and picked up BJ. "Let's go home and eat."

Back in Michigan Grandpa used to help me figure out what to do about burglars. Once we planned how to rig up a fence alarm in case someone broke into his field. And Grandpa even made a pretend door on one of the walls of his shop when I was real little. He rigged up all kinds of different locks all over it, so I could lock and unlock each one anytime I wanted.

Not now, though. Grandpa-was-not-in-a-good-mood. Neither was BJ. Not a very fun night, so far.

BJ's Tantrum

BJ rode back on Grandpa's shoulders. The sky was pink-purple. Almost dark.

Had Tyler and Trevor set up the tent yet? I HAD to figure out a way to get to the party! Mom didn't understand at all. You couldn't forget about a sleepover just because of a broken-down car.

Who could take me? Mom was stuck in some garage between Fullerton and Tustin, and Dad was on some highway, driving Grandpa's car here from Michigan. He wasn't supposed to get home till tomorrow. Where were parents when you needed them?

"Video!" BJ yelled, pointing to the video shop next to the Mini-mart. He started bouncing up and down, like Grandpa was a horse he could steer. "I want a video! I want my unicorns!" At home Mom always lets him pick his own cartoon video. He always picks the unicorn one. He knows right where it is. And he knows the whole video by heart.

"Grandpa's TV isn't here yet. We can't watch a video."

BJ's whole face crumpled. He started crying–his super-loud, nonstop screech. He doesn't howl like this very often. Mostly right before bedtime.

Poor Grandpa. Maybe his eardrums would explode that close to BJ's howl. I took one of the sandwiches out of the bag and handed it to BJ. "Here." Even if he didn't eat it, it might work like a plug. Then I pulled out a ham sandwich for me. It wasn't pizza. It sure wasn't birthday cake. But it was better than nothing.

"Grab me one, too," Grandpa said. We walked back to the apartment, chewing sandwiches. Grandpa was huffing a little. And walking sort of lopsided. Like his hip did hurt.

BJ didn't stop crying, even while he ate his sandwich. He swallowed and sniffled and made whiny noises all at the same time. He ate the middle out of both parts of his cheese sandwich. Then he dropped them. One part fell in

Grandpa's hair. The other part fell on the sidewalk. And BJ started winding up into his howl again.

The problem is, BJ doesn't really KNOW Grandpa, like I do. He only visited Grandpa once before. He probably doesn't even remember it. He was still in diapers back then.

BJ cried the whole way home. He didn't even stop when we walked into Grandpa's apartment and Grandpa set him down. BJ's terrible when he doesn't get a nap.

Grandpa was really huffing. And limping. He looked beat.

BJ kept howling.

If Dad were here, he would have said, "BJ's not a very happy camper."

If Mom were here, she would have said, "I know someone who's very tired and needs to go to bed."

Mom and Dad weren't here.

Grandpa didn't look like he was in good enough shape to do anything right now. He sagged into the only chair in the living room. He was really huffing.

BJ lay down on the floor and howled.

I desperately looked around the apartment.

What would make BJ stop crying? I started racking my brain. No toys, no TV, no videos, nothing to bribe him with. What DID this place have?

Then I thought of something. One thing the apartment DID have. "BJ," I said, leaning down close to his ear, with my best big brother authority, "it's time for your bath!"

No Way to Get There

I'm so smart. BJ was happy again, swishing around in the bathwater, blowing bubbles. He loves baths so much that usually Mom has to pull the plug to get him to come out. He didn't even mind that Grandpa doesn't have bath toys or bubble bath.

Now that BJ finally stopped screaming, I could check on the sleepover again. They better not have cut the cake!

"Never leave BJ alone in the bathroom." That's one of Mom's rules. I yanked the phone cord as far as it would go, so I could see in the bathroom doorway, while I dialed Tyler's number.

Tyler's mom answered the phone.

"Zach! We miss you. The boys are outside. I don't know if Tyler can come to the phone. Well, all right, if it's really important, I'll get him."

They probably WERE setting up the tent. It was getting dark. Half the evening was already gone.

Where was MOM? How long did it take to fix a car?

I poked my head in the bathroom. "You okay, BJ?"

"Yep." More glug and slosh sounds. He was playing "whale." Water was getting on the floor.

"Zach, are you going to come or not?" Tyler's voice spoke into the phone. "We can't wait anymore. We're setting up the tent and then we're going to cut the cake."

"Zach," Grandpa called, "that's not your mom on the phone, is it?"

"No. Just a friend," I answered. I turned back to the phone.

"My mom's car broke down. She's getting it fixed," I whispered into the receiver, so Grandpa wouldn't hear. I didn't want him to know how much I hated staying here. "She'll take me over as soon as it's fixed," I lied.

There was a pause. "Are you sure?" Tyler said. Then his voice changed. "I know! I should've thought of this before. My mom can come get you! It's not too far, is it?

That was a great idea! "It's one of the apartments across from the bowling alley. Number twelve," I said. "Do you really think she'll do that?" Then I looked at Grandpa. He was still sprawled in the one living room chair, still breathing hard. That trip to the Mini-mart and BJ's screaming had worn him out. Grandpa would not be able to take care of BJ by himself. Not unless BJ stayed in the bathtub all night, till he fell asleep. No wonder Mom and Dad had talked Grandpa into moving off the farm. He didn't have nearly as much energy as he used to. He looked so pooped right now.

DRAT!

"Look, Tyler, I guess . . . that won't work. I guess . . . I need to stay here till Mom gets here. Can you . . . wait another half hour?"

There was a long, mad sigh on the other end. "Okay. ONE more half hour. That's all. Deadbolts. Over and out."

"Signing off. Deadbolts."

One more half hour. Mom better get back by then.

Grandpa got up as I hung up the phone.

"Thank goodness for bathtubs," he said, putting his hands in the pockets of his bib overalls. "That was a great idea, Zach."

Grandpa peeked in at BJ, then walked over to the

patio door. He was still limping a little.

I got up and stood beside him. The backyard was so tiny. It was a cement patio, with some bushes and bark around the edges, near the fence. In Michigan, Grandpa's backyard was huge. And he had lots of apple trees. He made applesauce in the blender.

"It's July. Fireflies should be out," Grandpa said. His voice was gruff again.

Catching fireflies was one of the fun summer things to do at Grandpa's. I looked at his face. He looked sad. Just like I felt. "Hey, Grandpa, remember the time you tried to take a picture of fireflies in the field by your yard? And it got all blurry, even with the tripod?" I looked down at the boxes. "Are your photographs here, Grandpa?" Maybe looking at his pictures would cheer him up.

"They're in some box somewhere," Grandpa said in that same stiff, gruff voice. His arms were folded across his chest. He was still staring at the tiny backyard.

It was getting darker. I could hear noises from some of the other yards.

"You think any burglars could break in here, Grandpa?"

"There are good locks on the doors, Zach."

"Yeah, but what if a burglar hopped that fence? You

have a good lock on the FRONT door, but patio doors are easy to break into. You need to put special window-stops in them."

"Well, now, I think the security is fine here," Grandpa said, with the teeniest hint of a smile on his face.

There was a wail from the bathroom.

"I've got dinkles!" BJ hollered. "I'm all dinkled! Help!"

The Dinkle Bath

I forgot BJ! I forgot Mom's rule! I ran into the bathroom. Grandpa hurried behind me.

"Dinkles!" BJ yelled, holding out his hands, palms up. Tears ran down his face. "Look at all the dinkles!"

"What?" His hands looked all right to me. "What are you bawling about? There aren't any such things as dinkles!"

Grandpa knelt down beside the tub with a little grunt. "Show me the dinkles, BJ."

"Here. Right here. Look!" BJ pointed to his palms. "I'm all dinkled!" He started bawling again.

WRINKLES. That's what he was hollering about. His fingers were all scrunched up like raisins, from being in the bath so long. "It's from the bath–" I started, but Grandpa cut in.

"BJ, look at my hand. Think you're the only one with them dinkles? Look." Grandpa put his hand next to BJ's. Grandpa's hand was REALLY wrinkled. And it wasn't from bathwater.

BJ stopped crying. His eyes got big. He reached out and touched Grandpa's gnarled, old hand.

"You got dinkles, too?" he asked in a tiny voice.

"Sure do." Grandpa held out the other hand. Then he pointed to his neck and face. "See? All over. I have dinkles all over me, BJ."

"We both got dinkles," BJ said. He smiled, a great big BJ grin. He looked at me. "YOU don't have dinkles," he said. "Just Grandpa and ME do."

Grandpa started to reach up to the towel rack. "Oops, Zach, there aren't any towels. Go look through the boxes quick. BJ's got dinkles AND goose bumps. He's cold."

There wasn't an overhead light in the living room, like in the bathroom. It was hard to even read the labels on the boxes now. I finally found some kitchen towels and place mats and pot holders in the box of kitchen stuff. I grabbed

the whole pile and ran to the bathroom.

"Here. These are all I could find." I dumped them on the counter.

Grandpa looked at the pot holders and raised his eyebrows. He rummaged through the pile. "Well, what do you know?" He picked up a yellow-checkered kitchen towel with a grin. "A dinkle towel."

"Dinkle towels!" BJ clapped his hands and started to climb out of the tub. If I'd brought in those tiny little kitchen towels and tried to dry him off, he'd have started hollering and screaming for sure. But Grandpa saved the day–just the right thing to say.

He knew it, too. Grandpa looked very proud.

"Zach, better go check and see if you can find any more. These things are thin." Grandpa had already used two just on BJ's head and hair.

"Find more dinkle towels, Zach!" ordered BJ, standing there naked on the bare floor.

Brat. If we weren't stuck here at Grandpa's–if we were home, with Mom–I clamped my mouth shut and went back into the living room.

It was really getting dark. Must be late. And I was missing the whole sleepover. I grabbed the phone lying on the floor and pulled it into the living room. Good thing it had a lighted dial.

Tyler's mom answered again. "Zach! You're quite the phone caller today." She didn't sound too happy about that. "Well, I really can't call Tyler to the phone now. The boys are outside. Okay, I'll tell him you called. Bye, Zach."

She was sick of me calling.

So what was I supposed to do? How could I keep in touch with Tyler? Why didn't Mom show up?

Dinkle towels. That's what I was supposed to be finding. I looked around. The room was so dark now, it was hard to see anything even with the hall light and the kitchen light on. The only other lights were the holiday lights BJ had pulled out of the box of ornaments. I plugged them in. They didn't help much, lying on the floor. I laid the string over the mantel.

The living room was dark except for the tiny blinking lights over the fireplace. It was hard to see the rest of the room. There were only those tiny glowing lights. Everything else was dim, shadowy, and suddenly, almost–mysterious.

I KNEW that it was the middle of July. But something inside of me got that excited holiday feeling, seeing those blinking lights. The room didn't feel empty and boring anymore. Right then, it felt like the sort of room where anything could happen.

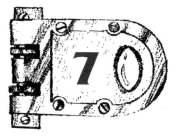

Running Out of Time

BJ was standing naked in the middle of the bathroom with his arms folded on his chest and a stubborn look on his face when I walked in.

"Not my SHIRT." BJ stomped his foot on one of the wet kitchen towels. "I'm supposed to wear my PJ's after I take my bath. Mommy always puts on my PJ's!"

"But BJ, there aren't any PJ's here." With a little grunt, Grandpa got up from his knees and looked around the bathroom. He pointed to the lightbulb. "See? No PJ's THERE." He pulled out one of the empty drawers. "See? No PJ's THERE." He scratched his head and looked into the bathtub where the water was still draining out. "No PJ's THERE."

This was more like it. Grandpa did stuff like this all the time in Michigan. I looked at him hopefully. Was he starting to be more like his old self again? BJ ran over to the toilet and flushed it. "No PJ's THERE," he cried. He turned on the sink faucets. "No PJ's THERE!" He ran out of the bathroom, almost slipping on the little towels and started down the hall. "No PJ's THERE." A second later I heard the squeal.

"Pretty lights!" BJ yelped.

Grandpa sort of sucked in his breath when he saw the room. He felt it, too. That mysterious hushed feeling, with the lights twinkling. . .

BJ wrecked it right away. He touched one of the little blinking lights. "No PJ's THERE!" Then he started pulling things out of the boxes. "No PJ's THERE, no PJ's THERE." He dumped more ornaments out of the decorations box.

"No, stop, wait," I yelled, running after him. He was all wound up again. How did Mom survive with him all day, every day?

"Get back in the bathroom! You need to put on clothes!"

Grandpa scooped him up. "Know what?" Grandpa

said. "Dinkles don't like to be cold. And sometimes," his voice got very low, "they like to wear shirts and shorts instead of PJ's."

Good old Grandpa. He really was getting with it again. The dinkles must have done it.

BJ stopped wriggling. He looked at Grandpa. "My dinkles ARE cold," he whispered. He pulled at his ear and yawned.

Usually about eight or nine o'clock every night, BJ suddenly goes from full speed to dead battery, and he konks. He was getting like that now, I could tell.

He didn't fuss at all when Grandpa scooped him up and took him back in the bathroom to dress him.

I looked at the phone lying on the hall floor.

I could make another call. . .

But Tyler's mom hadn't sounded too happy last time. She'd probably get mad. Then she wouldn't want me to come over at all.

It was really getting dark now. The stars were coming out. I peered into the shadows of the tiny backyard. Too bad there weren't fireflies, for Grandpa.

My eyes went to the top of the fence. I swallowed. You never knew who might be lurking in dark corners somewhere. It was a high fence, but that wouldn't stop a

criminal. If this were a TV show, someone would rig a burglar alarm right in the flower bed. Then, when the guy jumped the fence and landed in the geraniums, he'd probably set off the whole system. The alarm would go off at the central police headquarters. Five squad cars would come screaming down the street. The police would catch the guy red-handed.

Wow, what a story! It gave me shivery goose bumps, just thinking about it. COULD happen, too. Tyler and Trevor would love it.

Tyler and Trevor. The party. Had a half hour passed yet? How late could someone show up to a sleepover? My eyes went to my bare wrist. Why did I forget to wear my watch today?

Where was MOM? The night was going fast. If I didn't get there soon, I wouldn't get there at all.

The Three Little Pigs and the Reindeer-Unicorn

Grandpa was looking through the boxes when I walked back inside. "BJ's all ready for bed. He just needs a place to sleep. Seems to me I wrapped some of the breakable things in blankets—"

He pulled out a bundle from the kitchen box. "What did I tell you? My green bed blanket. Would you help me spread this out, Zach?"

The blanket took up half the living room. Grandpa pulled out a big wad of foam, with bumps all over it like an egg carton. "Your mattress, BJ!" And he slid the foam under the edge of the green blanket. "Just like camping."

BJ rubbed his eyes. He stepped on the padded foam. "It feels funny," he said in a tired, yawny voice. Then he pulled on his ear.

"Lie down," Grandpa said softly. "We're camping and this is your special camp bed." He patted the foam.

BJ lay down. He turned over on his back, then flopped on his stomach, then sat up again.

"I didn't see the rest of my unicorn show." He rubbed his eyes hard.

Poor BJ. He was REALLY tired. Good thing I didn't sneak off and leave Grandpa alone with him. When BJ gets like this, you need two people, at least.

"Lie down on your special camp bed." Grandpa patted the foam again. "Hey, BJ, feel–this bed's got dinkles!" He ran his hand over the egg-carton bumps.

"Dinkles?" BJ patted the bumps, too. "Is it a dinkle bed?" He yawned again. The tired part of him was fighting with the bratty part of him. It was really dark in the living room, with just the twinkling lights. And he'd had a bath. If he'd been home right now, he'd have konked out in two seconds. He couldn't even keep his eyes all the way open.

"I want my unicorn," he whispered.

"How about a story?" Grandpa said.

"Good idea!" I grabbed a pamphlet sitting on the top

of the kitchen box, "Parts and Service Manual for Your Refrigerator." I started reading. "Once upon a time there were three little pigs . . ." There was a big picture of a refrigerator on the pamphlet.

"And each little pig built his house out of something different. Like bricks and branches and stuff." A diagram of the refrigerator parts stared at me. "The bricks were the strongest. They even had a five year warranty on some of the parts. And then along came this wolf. His name was, um, Crisper. And he said, 'Little pig, little pig, let me come in . . .'

"Anyway, it wasn't just wolves they had to worry about. There were burglars hanging around, too. Even bricks probably wouldn't be good enough. Those pigs should have used deadbolts . . ." I grinned.

Was BJ listening? I peeked at him. His eyes were closed. His thumb was in his mouth. His fingers were rubbing the satin edge of Grandpa's green blanket.

"So the wolf said, 'I'll huff and puff and blow your house down.'" I went on, making my voice softer and softer, instead of louder and louder, like the wolf's voice should get. I peeked at BJ again. Eyes closed. Breathing deep. Asleep. FINALLY. I shut the pamphlet.

Grandpa was bent over one of the boxes, working on

something with his glue gun.

Suddenly he held up a plastic reindeer with a big grin. It had a long icicle ornament attached to its head.

"He wanted to see a unicorn before he'd go to sleep," Grandpa said, with a proud smile. "I thought in case your story didn't work, we'd have backup." He turned the reindeer-unicorn in his hand, studying it.

"I think the icicle's a bit low. I'll try again. There are more reindeer in the decorations box, and there's a whole package of icicle ornaments." He pulled out another plastic reindeer, grabbed another icicle, and held up his glue gun. "Right, there." He stuck the icicle to the reindeer's head.

"Reindeer-unicorns!" I started giggling. It looked so funny, with brown reindeer antlers and a clear, pointed horn coming out of the top of its head. If it weren't for the reindeer antlers, it probably would have looked like a unicorn.

"Not bad. Not bad at all." Grandpa looked really pleased with himself. "I think they look much better with a horn. I'm going to turn the lot of them into unicorns." He picked up several reindeer and his glue gun and headed for the kitchen. "The light's much better out here."

I yawned and leaned back against a box. It felt so late.

In this dark, quiet room with the twinkling lights, Tyler's party was starting to feel so far away.

Tiny blinking lights. On and off. On and off. Sort of like . . . fireflies. Grandpa would have really liked it if they were fireflies. July was their best month in Michigan.

Suddenly I had an idea.

California Fireflies

I glanced into the kitchen. Grandpa was bent over the table, with his back to me.

Were there more strings of little blinking lights in the box of decorations?

Yes! One nice long one. I picked up the string of lights and tiptoed over to the patio, sliding the door very slowly and quietly, so Grandpa wouldn't hear.

Good thing there was an overhead patio light, so I could see what I was doing. I finally found the outlet, with its hinged metal cover to protect it from rain. I plugged in the string of lights, then stretched the wire over the bushes at the edge of the patio. There was still string left, so I wound it in and out of the geraniums.

I turned off the overhead patio light.

Tiny yellow lights blinked on the bush and flashed among the dark flowers.

They DID look sort of like fireflies! Grandpa would love them!

Grandpa was putting a horn on the last reindeer when I tiptoed back into the kitchen. Six reindeer-unicorns stood in line on the kitchen counter.

"The whole herd's done," he said proudly. "All ready for BJ, when he wakes up."

"Come here, Grandpa," I whispered. "I want to show you something." I tugged on his arm, pulling him over to the patio door.

"Ta-dah!" I spread my arm out toward the lights. "Fireflies, Grandpa! We DO have them in California!" I started giggling. I couldn't help it. I was so excited. It was even darker now and some of those lights really did look like fireflies. Especially the ones in the geraniums.

"Well, I'll be," Grandpa said softly. The same kind of voice he used when he and I would find something really neat hidden in the woods on our walks.

"Well, I'll be," Grandpa said again. He looked at me–

a long look, with a little smile at the corners of his mouth. "Fireflies in California, after all."

"Yep," I said and giggled again. I put my hand over my mouth, to muffle the sounds. I did NOT want BJ to wake up. "July's their best month, right, Grandpa? That's why there are so many of them." I slid open the patio door and pulled Grandpa out with me. "Come on, take a good look at them."

Grandpa looked around the yard. I knew what he was thinking.

"Not a very big yard, is it?" I said.

"Firefly-sized," Grandpa said.

"Grandpa . . . do you . . . hate this new apartment?" The words just burst out. I didn't plan them.

There was a silence. It felt really long. Finally Grandpa reached down and touched one of the little blinking lights on one of the geraniums. "Not as much as I did a few hours ago," Grandpa said.

He put his arm around my shoulder. "Now I've seen California fireflies." Another grin. "Thanks, Zach."

I started to slide the patio door open, then froze.

There was a strange thumping sound coming from the other side of the fence.

The Break-in

"Grandpa, did you hear that?" I grabbed his shirt-sleeve with one hand, while my other hand pointed toward the fence. "Someone's out there," I mouthed the words.

Another noise. The swishing sounds of footsteps in the grass. Then a small clatter.

I stared at the fence. My fingers were cemented to the material of Grandpa's shirt. "Get down, Grandpa! Get down!"

But Grandpa didn't crouch down to hide. He stood very straight, with a watchful frown on his face.

There was a thud, like something falling. I clapped my hand over my mouth.

It was finally happening. A real burglary. Someone was trying to get into Grandpa's yard! I told him this place needed better security!

"In, in," I whispered, pulling frantically on Grandpa's shirtsleeve. "Call the police. Call 9-l-l. Hurry!"

Instead, Grandpa put his finger to his lips and took one step forward, toward the fence.

"No!" I tried to pull him back. My blood was on a race-track, pumping furiously. Even my whisper was high and squeaky. "There's too many of them!" I don't know how I knew that. I just did. It worked that way in most of the movies.

"Shh . . ." Grandpa took another step toward the fence.

Oh boy, oh boy, this was not good. Grandpa was over seventy, and I was nine and a half. I bet the guy on the other side of the fence was probably six foot four.

He wasn't alone, either! I heard muffled voices, scampering sounds, another small thud against the fence. Like . . . someone's foot . . . kicking. Or . . . trying to climb up.

Every single thing I ever learned to do in case of a robbery turned to mush in my brain. I stood there, frozen as a statue. In my imagination, I was running into the apartment, plunging right through the screen door without even bothering to open it, grabbing the phone, dialing 9-1-1. "Police, police, there's been a burglary . . ." My voice was loud, firm. "Yes, apartment twelve . . ."

I could hear it, see it, feel it. I just couldn't DO it.

Grandpa took another cautious step toward the fence. His foot brushed one of the firefly lights. I clenched my fists so tight that even my stubby, chewed-off fingernails felt like claws jabbing me.

Another thud against the fence. For one quick moment, I could see someone clinging to the top of the shadowed fence; the hands and the top of a head were just barely visible. Something hurtled out of the darkness and fell on the geraniums.

"Grandpa!" I yelled, grabbing his arm. "It might be some kind of bomb. Touch it and you explode. Get back. Don't touch it!"

I heard running sounds. They were getting away. Those seven-foot burglars who'd dropped a bomb in our yard were making a getaway. We had to DO SOMETHING!

"It's not a bomb, Zach. It's a box." Grandpa leaned over and carefully pushed back the plants, squinting into the geraniums. He didn't look a bit scared. Just curious, businesslike, matter-of-fact, like when he checked the vegetables in his farm garden. It took more than bombs and seven-foot burglars to scare Grandpa. He was tough.

"Be careful, Grandpa!" He hadn't watched nearly as many shows about burglaries as I had. He didn't know the possibilities. "We should call the police," I cried. "Right away, so they can catch them before they get away! Do you hear me, Grandpa? Don't touch it! They'll want to take fingerprints!"

"Just a second." Grandpa reached down to the half-crumpled box.

My heart was going so fast I could hardly breathe. But I took a small step forward. I couldn't be a chicken, when Grandpa was being so brave. Anyway, part of me wanted to see it, too. I mean, how often does a person have strange things fly over his fence so late at night?

"Oh, Grandpa, be careful!"

Slowly Grandpa picked up the bent white box and set it on the cement patio. He opened it.

"Cake?" his voice slid up into a surprised question. His eyes got big. "By golly, it IS cake!" He held the box out so I could see it. "Someone dropped cake in our yard, Zach."

By the patio light, I could see vanilla cake with chocolate frosting. It had probably been three or four pieces to start with. A lot of the frosting was stuck to the sides of the box. Cakes weren't meant to be tossed over fences.

I knew. Even before I saw the paper stuck to the side of the box and pulled it off and saw the big words printed in felt pen: "The Deadbolts were here."

The voices, the whispering, the scuffling, the thuds, the flying cake.

The Deadbolts were here.

"My . . . friends," I whispered, looking from the smushed cake to Grandpa's surprised face.

"Your friends did this?" Grandpa echoed. He looked down at the smushed cake, then back to me. "But, why?"

"It's Tyler's birthday, and they must have ridden their bikes over." How had they managed that, without Tyler's mom finding out? And finding this apartment, in the dark?

"I see." Grandpa sounded like he really didn't see. "Why didn't they knock at the front door?"

"Well, because . . . because . . ."

Because they were the DEADBOLTS. That's why. They wanted to try a first-class joke break-in. And they did a great job!

"They're pretty good burglars, huh, Grandpa?"

"Ah," said Grandpa in a whole different voice, "now I get it. More burglar stuff, eh? And you've got your friends

in on it, too."

"Yep." I was a little bit shaky still, from the scare. But I couldn't stop the big grin that felt like it went all the way to my ears. Of course, mostly our club is about stopping burglars, not being burglars. But it was a great prank.

I reached into the box and scooped out some icing with my finger. Tasted great, too!

Well, I had told them not to cut the cake without me.

The Deadbolts Were Here

"Not bad cake," said Grandpa. He licked the icing from his fingers. We were sitting on the floor of the living room, leaning over the box, trying not to get the crumbly, smushed pieces on the green blanket. Beside us, BJ snored softly. The little lights twinkled from the mantel.

Smushed or not, the cake tasted terrific. I scraped the last blob of icing from the sides of the box and licked it off my finger. "Well, that's it," I whispered. "We ate the whole thing, Grandpa."

It gave me shivers every time I thought of it flying through the air and landing like a UFO in the backyard. I was so proud of Tyler and Trevor. It must have been real tricky for them to sneak away on their bikes so late and find Grandpa's apartment. I hoped they'd made it back without getting caught.

I'd call first thing in the morning and find out. Too late now.

And . . . too late to go over there.

I knew it for sure now. I didn't need a watch to tell me. My fuzzy, tired head told me loud and clear.

And not just my head. Suddenly I was so tired I could crash right down beside BJ and start snoring, too. How late was it? All my usual ways of telling time were gone: clocks, TV shows, radio. We didn't have any of those things. Just this dark room, and my stomach full of delicious cake, and those lights twinkling from the mantel.

"It's getting late. You should try to get some sleep, too, Zach." Grandpa tried to get up, with a little grunt. He couldn't quite do it. He kept sagging back.

"Here, Grandpa, I'll help you up." I got up and held out my hand.

"And we'll be in a fine fix if I pull YOU over."

He almost did. That started us both giggling. "What would I do without you, Zach?" Grandpa said as he struggled to his feet. He looked a little embarrassed. "Just let me catch my breath a minute, then we'll find you a piece of dinkle foam, too. Aha!" He pulled out a skinny piece and slid it under the green blanket next to BJ.

"There you go. And look, there's one for me, too." Grandpa lay his piece on my other side. "Fiddlesticks," he muttered. "After all that trouble getting up, now I have to get back down again. Better make sure I have everything I need."

My foam was okay, except that my feet stuck out over the end. It was hard to get comfortable. I tried lying on my back, my left side, my right side, my stomach, the works. I was so tired I couldn't go to sleep. Hard to relax in a strange place.

"Grandpa, did you lock the doors?"

"Yep."

"But the patio door's open."

"We need the air," said Grandpa. "It's warm in here."

"But–"

"Zach, don't worry. Like I said, this place has security."

"But Grandpa, if Tyler and Trevor could do an almost-break-in, then anybody could. What if some real robbers hopped the back fence, and got into the yard, and came in through our patio door?"

"They'd never make it to our patio fence. Someone

would catch them first."

"No one caught Tyler and Trevor." I stared out at the darkness that was Grandpa's patio. "What would we do, Grandpa?"

"Well, then," Grandpa made his voice low and fierce, "it'd be up to us to deal with them, Zach."

I turned onto my stomach. "How?"

"We could booby trap them. As a matter of fact we could do that ahead of time, before they even have a chance to case the joint." Grandpa pulled out the trusty old decorations box again and looked through it. He yanked out a leather strap that had half-a-dozen bells attached to it. They started ringing as he pulled it out.

Grandpa cupped his hand over them. "Shh," he told them. "BJ's sleeping." He turned to me.

"Now, watch." With another groan, he struggled up from the floor and went over to the patio door. He hung the leather strap by its loop from the door handle. "See, Zach? Any burglar coming in that way will set off our alarm," Grandpa said. Then he pulled the phone over beside us on our green blanket. "There. The second the bells start ringing, we lift the receiver and dial 9-l-l. How's that?"

"Not fast enough." I leaned on my elbows, staring around the room. "Until the police get here, we're at their

mercy, Grandpa. We have to have a plan B, in case the police aren't fast enough."

Grandpa reached out and turned the reindeer-unicorns
around, so that they were all facing the patio door. Their
horns pointed at it like weapons. "There. The cavalry will
scare them off."

I grinned through a yawn. "I don't think so." I tried to
plump up my piece of foam and lay back down on my
stomach. The lights blinked from across the room, soft and
sparkly. BJ was still snoring. Slowly, carefully, Grandpa
lowered himself onto his foam. "Ah, I made it."

"Pull the phone closer," I whispered. "We need it right
beside us."

"Yeah, you're right." Grandpa put it two inches from
our heads.

I reached down and pulled some of the extra part of the
green blanket over me. I plumped up the foam piece again.

"How are you doing, Zach?"

"Fine," I whispered back.

It was true. I was fine. It hadn't turned out to be such a
bad night, after all. I had my cake, I had my break-in, and
I even had a sort of sleepover.

"Grandpa?"

"Hmm?"

"What did you mean when you said you don't hate this place as much as you did a few hours ago?"

"Well, you see," Grandpa said softly, "after tonight, when I walk out onto the patio, I'll think—fireflies. And when I look at the fence, I'll think—cake. And whenever I get in the bathtub, I'll think—dinkles!"

His voice was starting to sound far away. It was those lights, blinking like that. They relaxed me so much. They still gave me that magical holiday feeling; they gave it to the whole room.

* * *

I dreamed that there was a herd of reindeer trying to get over the back fence and I was throwing gumdrops at them. The reindeer were making a lot of noise. One of them had an alarm that was ringing and ringing.

It was the phone. Right beside my head. I jerked up, trying to focus. BJ moaned and threw his arm out.

Then I heard Grandpa's voice, talking softly. "Yes? Well, that's good. No, you don't need to come by this late, Jenny. The boys are asleep anyway. Go home and get some sleep and come in the morning." He got gruffer. "I told you, we're FINE. Yes. See you in the morning."

"Was that Mom?" I mumbled, squinting in the darkness.

61

"Yeah," Grandpa whispered. "The car's fixed. She'll be here in the morning."

BJ flopped over again. Then he sat up in a wobbly sort of way. He opened his eyes. He saw the reindeer-unicorns first. He smiled, a sleepy smile. Then he looked at the twinkling lights, and at me and Grandpa.

"Merry Christmas," he mumbled and went back to sleep.

Through a sleepy haze, I grinned at Grandpa. The tiny lights twinkled above us, like magic.

Funny, but even though it's the middle of July, it feels sort of like . . . BJ's right.

Signing off. Deadbolts.